For Christopher and Kate Willis –J. W.

For Arik –T. R.

G. P. Putnam's Sons, a division of Penguin Putnam Books
for Young Readers, 345 Hudson Street, New York, NY 10014.
G. P. Putnam's Sons, Reg. U.S. Pat. & Tm. Off.
Published simultaneously in England by Andersen Press Ltd.
Published simultaneously in Canada.
Printed in Italy.
Designed by Gina DiMassi. Text set in Dom Casual.
L. C. Number: 00-023940
ISBN 0-399-23595-7
1 3 5 7 9 10 8 6 4 2
First Impression

WHAT DID I LOOK LIKE WHEN I WAS A BABY?

JEANNE WILLIS
illustrated by TONY ROSS

G. P. Putnam's Sons New York

"Mom . . . ," said Michael, "what did I look like when I was a baby?"

"You looked just like your grandpa," she said, smiling. "Bald and wrinkly!"

Far away in the jungle, the son of a baboon asked his mother the same question.

"Mom, what did I look like when I was a baby?"

"Pretty much the same as you do now," she said, "only not so hairy. You were a silly little monkey."

"I wonder what I looked like when I was a baby?" said the hippopotamus.

"The same as you do now, only smaller," said his mother. "Of course, you weighed a ton even then."

"What about me, Ma?" asked the leopard.

"You've always had spots," she said, "but your legs have grown much longer. It runs in the family."

"What did I look like when I was a baby?" asked the ostrich.

"Yo . . . Ma! Did I look like you when I was a runt?" asked the hyena.

"Fluffy? Ssssss . . . certainly not," she hissed. "You've always had beautiful sssskin. You were a ssscaled-down version of me."

"Nah!" she said. "You looked just like your dad and we laughed and laughed and laughed and laughed!"

"What about me?" asked the warthog. "Did I look like Father?"

"Rather!" snorted his mother. "Only he was an *enormous* boar."

"And me?" asked the chameleon. "Have I always looked like this, Mom?"

"Yes," she said. "The only thing that's changed is your color. . . . Oh, there you go again!"

So, one by one, all around the world, the animals learned that when they were babies, they looked like little versions of their moms and dads, pretty much. **UNTIL...**

"Mom . . . . . . ?" wondered the bullfrog.
"Son," she said, "don't even ask!"

But the little bullfrog went on and on: "Mom, what did I look like when I was a baby? What did I look like when I was a baby? What did I look like when I was a baby . . . ?" Until, in the end, his mother showed him a photograph.

"That's you when you were three weeks old," she said.

He stared at the photograph in horror. "Me?" he said. "That's not me! It looks nothing like a frog!"

Angry and confused, he hid under a stone and decided never to trust his mother again.

Suddenly, he heard all his brothers and sisters singing:

"Little bullfrog babies
Don't look like frogs at all,
They're small and black and slimy,
And they cannot hop or crawl,
A great big head, two dots for eyes,
A mouth just like an 'O,'
A tadpole tail that swims behind them
Everywhere they go.
But then they grow two kicking legs,
Two tiny, webby feet,
And then two perfect little arms
With fingers all complete,
Their tails shrink, they take a gulp
And climb onto a log,
And that is how a baby tadpole
Turns into a frog!"

When the little bullfrog realized all the frogs in the world were once tadpoles, he felt much happier.

"I know what I looked like when I was a baby!" he said, smiling.

"Beautiful!" said his mother.

THE BULLFROG SONG
Music by Christopher Willis
Words by Jeanne Willis
(can also be sung to the tune of "Miss Lucy Had a Steamboat")

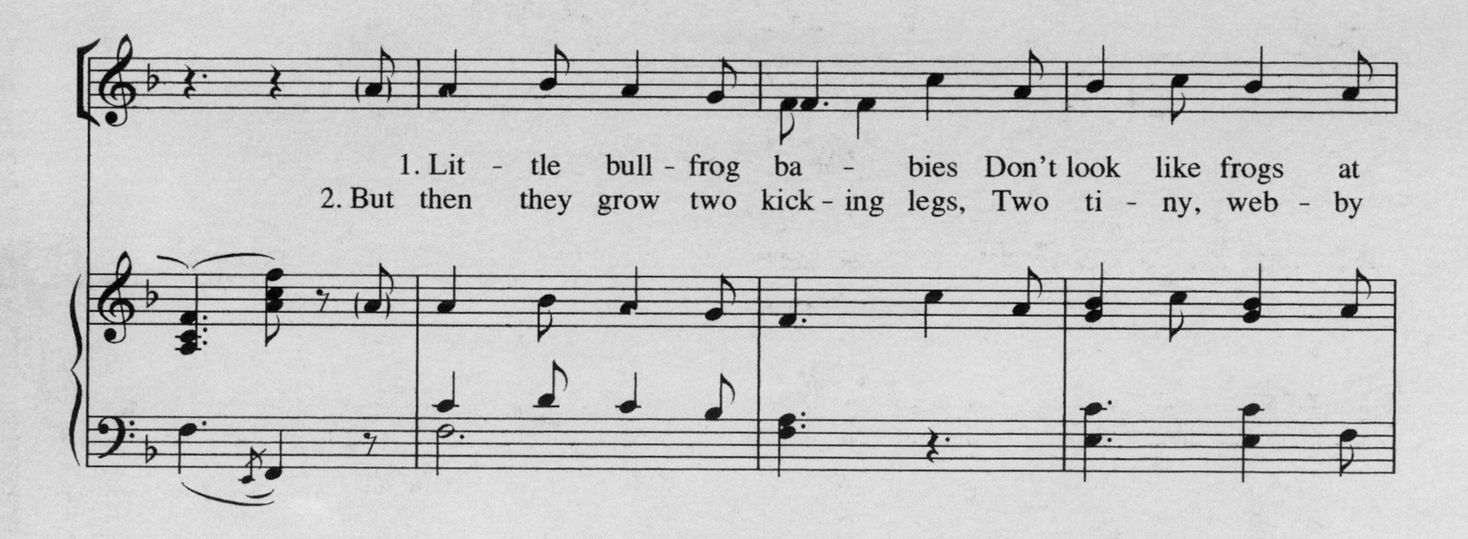
1. Lit - tle bull - frog ba - bies Don't look like frogs at
2. But then they grow two kick - ing legs, Two ti - ny, web - by

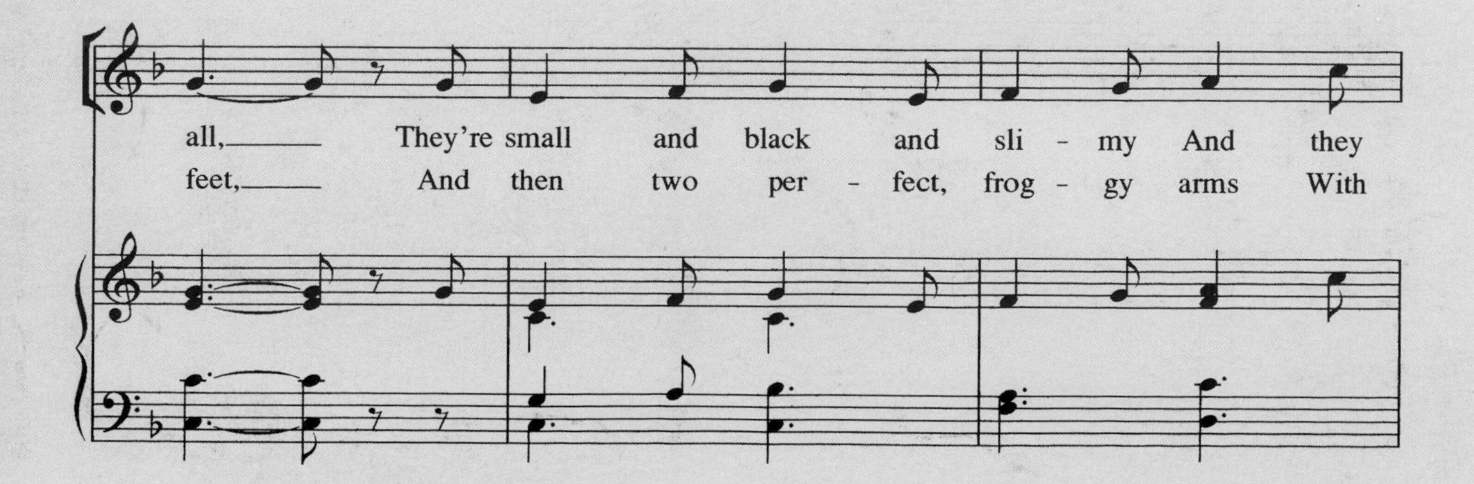
all, They're small and black and sli - my And they
feet, And then two per - fect, frog - gy arms With